# The Legend of Sleepy Hollow

Adapted by Freya Littledale
from the story by Washington Irving

Illustrated by Melanie W. Hall

SCHOLASTIC INC.
New York  Toronto  London  Auckland  Sydney

ISBN 0-590-45050-6

Text copyright © 1992 by Freya Littledale.
Illustrations copyright © 1992 by Melanie W. Hall.
All rights reserved. Published by Scholastic Inc.

12 11 10 9 8 7 6 5 4 3 2 1    2 3 4 5 6 7/9

Printed in the U.S.A.                    23

First Scholastic printing, October 1992

For Beatrice de Regniers —F.L.
For Frank and Dorothy Hall with love —M.W.H.

Not far from the village of Tarrytown
lies a quiet little valley that has always been
one of the most enchanted places on earth.
It is known as Sleepy Hollow.

The very land itself seems to cast a spell
over the people, who move and speak
as if they were in a dream.
They hear strange music and voices in the air.
And they whisper of ghosts and goblins
that haunt the valley.

The most fearsome ghost of all
is the horseman without a head.
Some say his head was carried away
by a cannonball during the Revolutionary War,
and the ghost won't rest until he finds it.
So every night he rides to the battleground
in search of his missing head.
At dawn he returns to the graveyard
where he was buried.

People still huddle together around a crackling fire
and tell tales of this phantom
called the Headless Horseman of Sleepy Hollow.

Long ago, a schoolmaster named Ichabod Crane
came from Connecticut
to teach the children of Sleepy Hollow.
Tall and skinny, with narrow shoulders
and a small, flat head,
he looked as if he were pinned together.
His arms were like noodles
dangling from his sleeves
while his feet were as huge as shovels.
Striding along on a windy day,
with his clothes fluttering in the breeze,
he could have been mistaken for a scarecrow
just escaped from a cornfield.

ICHABOD

ABCDEFGHIJKLMNOPQR

His one-room schoolhouse, built of logs,
was in a lonely spot at the foot of a hill.
Close by, a brook murmured
while his students mumbled their ABCs.
Sometimes, Ichabod commanded,
"Pay attention!"
And if a lazy pupil failed to do as he was told,
Ichabod spanked the offender
with a birch switch.
"Spare the rod and spoil the child,"
he always said.
Ichabod's pupils were never spoiled.

S T U V W X Y Z & · 1 2 3 4 5 6 7 8 9 0

But Ichabod Crane was not an unkind man.
Indeed, after school, he often went home
with some of his students —
especially if their mothers were skilled
in the art of cooking.
You see, his wages were small.
And though he was very skinny,
he had the appetite of a bear.
So Ichabod spent many afternoons
stuffing himself with cakes,
and puddings, and pies
which the good mothers happily made for him.

Aside from eating,
one of Ichabod's greatest pleasures
was reading tales of ghosts and witches.
On sunny days, he often stretched out
on a bed of clover near the brook
and read until dusk.
The tales were as real
and necessary to him as food.
On each page, he found delicious, scary morsels.

But when he made his way through the woods
back to the farmhouse where he was staying,
every sound startled him.
Even the trees seemed to reach out
their branches to grab him.

"Sleepy Hollow is bewitched," Ichabod told himself.
"Still, I will not be afraid.
My voice will drive away
all evil spirits that dwell here —
even the Headless Horseman."

Then Ichabod began to sing so loudly,
the people of the valley
could hear him as they sat
by their doors in the evening.
And they were quick to say,
"Aye, the schoolmaster has a wonderful voice!"

Almost everyone admired the schoolmaster.
"He reads books from beginning to end,"
said one farmer's wife.

"He knows many tales of witchcraft,"
said another.

"He sings like a nightingale," sighed a third.

"And I have some news,"
announced the best cook in the group.
"In exchange for my plum pudding,
he's going to give me singing lessons."

"Singing lessons!" cried the others.
"We want them, too!"

Ichabod didn't know it,
but his troubles were about to begin.
Until then, his life had been fairly pleasant.
For a week at a time,
he lived at the homes of his pupils.
There, he mended fences and cut wood for the fire.
He even helped take care of the children.
He could sit with a child on his knee,
rock a cradle with one huge foot,
and sing song after song without stopping.

When Ichabod agreed to give singing lessons,
the women were delighted.
They gathered around him,
and Ichabod led them in song.
After the lessons, they told ghostly tales
while a row of apples
roasted and sputtered on the hearth.
They felt cozy and safe together.

But Ichabod didn't feel cozy or safe
during his lonely walks home.
A snow-covered bush could be a ghost.
Any sound could be footsteps.
The footsteps could belong to a stranger.
And the stranger could be the Headless Horseman.

Yet, the Headless Horseman and all
other ghosts were terrors of the night
that disappeared in daylight.
And, in spite of such horrors,
Ichabod might have remained a contented man.

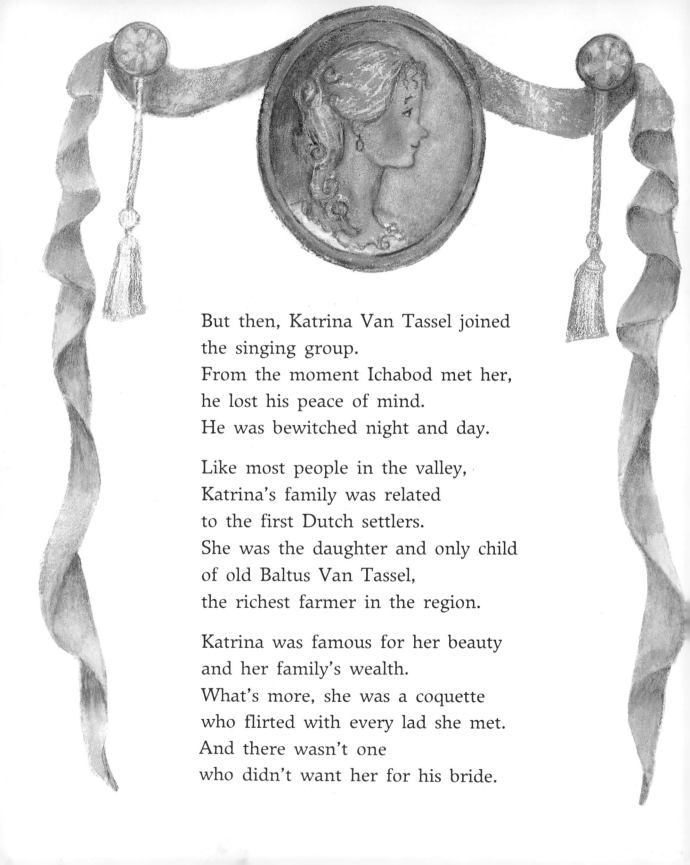

But then, Katrina Van Tassel joined
the singing group.
From the moment Ichabod met her,
he lost his peace of mind.
He was bewitched night and day.

Like most people in the valley,
Katrina's family was related
to the first Dutch settlers.
She was the daughter and only child
of old Baltus Van Tassel,
the richest farmer in the region.

Katrina was famous for her beauty
and her family's wealth.
What's more, she was a coquette
who flirted with every lad she met.
And there wasn't one
who didn't want her for his bride.

But until she met Ichabod Crane,
Katrina's favorite suitor was Brom Van Brunt.
This local hero was celebrated throughout the region
for his great skill on horseback.
He was broad-shouldered and double jointed,
with curly black hair
and a twinkle in his eyes.
Known for his mischief as well as his strength,
he was nicknamed Brom Bones.
Brom was always ready for a good fight,
or a good laugh.

Sometimes he and his gang, the Sleepy Hollow Boys,
rode past the farmhouses in the dead of night.
"Whoopee-eee!" they shouted.
The good people, awakened from their sleep,
just smiled and shook their heads.
"Brom Bones and his friends
are having fun tonight!" they said.
No matter what Brom did,
they couldn't help admiring him.

With a rival like Brom,
most men would have given up hope
of winning a lady's love.
But Ichabod was unlike most men.

"I will give Katrina
private singing lessons," he decided.
"And I will pick a bouquet of daisies
and snapdragons just for her."
With bouquet in hand,
the schoolmaster found his way
to the Van Tassel mansion.
It was nestled in a cove
on the shores of the Hudson River.

Nearby, Ichabod saw the barn
that seemed to burst with pigs,
geese, turkeys, and chickens.
When he entered the house,
his eyes were dazzled
by pewter mugs, silver candlesticks,
and mahogany tables that shone like mirrors.
He pictured himself lord and master
of this grand estate.
He had only to win Katrina,
who was the lady of his dreams.

So he visited her every week.
And every week, after the singing lessons,
Ichabod wooed Katrina
on their little twilight walks.

"My dear," he'd say, "you are prettier
than all the flowers in the valley."

"You don't mean it," Katrina said.

"Oh, but I do," Ichabod assured her.

For Katrina
Love, Ichabod

Of course, Brom Bones knew of these visits,
and he was eager to fight his rival.
"I will double the schoolmaster up
and stuff him on a shelf
in his own schoolhouse," he announced.

But Ichabod realized he could never
win a fight with Brom Bones,
and he was very careful to stay out of his way.
So Brom was forced to play practical jokes
on the schoolmaster.

He smoked out the singing class
by stopping up the chimney.
He and his gang broke
into the schoolhouse at night
and turned everything topsy-turvy.
Ichabod blamed it on witches.

But the most vexing prank of all
was when Brom trained his dog to whine
while Ichabod gave Katrina voice lessons.
"It's the witches again," said Ichabod.
Katrina just giggled.

*Mr. Crane, you are invited to a Harvest Festival*

Now, one day in late autumn,
a messenger came to the schoolhouse.
"Sir," said he, "you are invited
to a harvest festival at the home of the Van Tassels
this very evening."
With these words, the messenger bowed and left.

Ichabod hurried the students
through their lessons
and dismissed them an hour early.
Then he announced to the empty room,
"Tonight I will ask Katrina to be my wife."

Ichabod spent an extra hour dressing
in his best, and indeed only, black suit.
After combing his straggly hair,
he put on a little woolen hat.
Then he smiled at himself
in a bit of broken mirror.
"Remember, Ichabod Crane," he said.
"This is your night!"

Ichabod borrowed a plow-horse from Hans Van Ripper,
with whom he was staying.
The horse, called Gunpowder,
was blind in one eye, shaggy,
and broken down.
But Ichabod didn't seem to mind.
He felt like a knight
on his way to his lady's castle.
Indeed, he was the perfect rider for such a steed.
His knees and elbows stuck out
like a grasshopper's
while his arms resembled flapping wings.

It was a glorious afternoon,
and Ichabod feasted his eyes on the trees
in their bright fall costumes
of gold, orange, purple, and scarlet.
He practiced proposing to Katrina.
"Will you marry me, my dearest?
Will you be my wife?"

Robins and bluejays twittered in the bushes,
and they all seemed to call, "I will! I will!"

As Ichabod jogged along,
his stomach rumbled with hunger.
He pictured apple pies and pumpkin pies,
honey cakes and fruit cakes,
glazed hams and candied yams.
He imagined pigs fully roasted
with apples in their mouths,
while turkeys, stuffed with chestnuts,
lay on pillows of cranberry sauce.
Such thoughts were enough to make him smack his lips.

Once Ichabod arrived at the festival,
he wasn't disappointed.
His eyes rolled when he saw the food,
and his spirits rose with each mouthful.

When the music began, he turned to Katrina.
"My dear," he said, "may I have the honor
of this dance?"

Katrina blushed and said, "Yes."

So the fiddler played
while everyone danced.
But all eyes were on Ichabod
who was as proud of his dancing
as he was of his singing.

The schoolmaster was the very picture
of rhythm with his arms and legs
and even his eyebrows
moving in time to the music.
He smiled at Katrina
and she smiled at him
while Brom Bones sat
alone in the corner.

When the dancing ended,
Ichabod went out on the porch
and listened to ghostly tales
told in hushed voices
as if they were secrets.

"I never used to believe in ghosts,"
said an old farmer named Brouwer.
"But now I do because I've seen one.
Yes, just last week,
I saw the Headless Horseman himself.
In fact, I rode behind him
until he reached the haunted bridge.
You won't believe what happened next."

"What?" asked Baltus Van Tassel.
"At the bridge," Brouwer whispered,
"the Horseman turned into a skeleton
and vanished over the treetops.
Then, even though it was a starlit night,
I heard a clap of thunder
and saw a flash of lightning."

Everyone was quiet until Brom Bones spoke.
"My horse, Daredevil, can beat
that goblin horse any time."
No one doubted his words.
Brom was the finest horseman in the land.

"I met the Headless Horseman
a few weeks ago," Brom continued.
"I even spoke to him.
'I'll race you for a bowl of punch,' I said.
So off we galloped until we reached the bridge.
I was ahead all the way —
so he still owes me that bowl of punch.
Anyway, the moment we got to the bridge,
the Horseman vanished in a flash of fire."

"Aye," Brouwer nodded.
"He always vanishes at the haunted bridge."

Ichabod didn't miss a word of these stories.
But he couldn't be outdone
by the likes of Brom Bones.
So he told scary tales of witchcraft
that he had heard in his native Connecticut.
Then he spoke of phantoms
he'd seen in Sleepy Hollow.
There were phantoms that howled in the night
and phantoms that stood still
and silent as statues near a giant tulip tree.

Soon the party began to break up.
Families gathered in their wagons
and headed home.
But Ichabod stayed behind
so he could speak privately to Katrina.
Again he assured himself,
"Tonight she will accept my proposal."

But something must have gone wrong
because Ichabod didn't stay long.
No one knows what really happened or why.
Perhaps Katrina had encouraged the schoolmaster
just to make Brom Bones jealous.
She was such a coquette,
anything was possible.

It was the very witching hour of the night
when the heartbroken Ichabod
began his journey home.
There wasn't a sign of life
for miles around.
The cheerful and familiar path
suddenly became strange to him.
Now and then, he heard the howl of a dog
or the groan of a bullfrog.

Ichabod's mind reeled with tales
of ghosts — especially the Headless Horseman.
The night grew darker and darker
as all the stars seemed to sink
deeper into the sky.
Slow-moving clouds soon hid
them all from sight.
Poor Ichabod had never felt so alone.

The twisted limbs of the old tulip tree
groaned and swayed in the wind.
Ichabod whistled to fight his fear.
He was certain the tree whistled back.

At that very moment,
Ichabod noticed, in the distance,
a gigantic, shadowy *thing*.
The thing did not move.
It seemed to be a monstrous shadow
that was part of the gloom.

Ichabod's hair rose up
on his head with terror.
"What can I do?" he whispered.
"It's too late for me to escape!"
Then he took a deep breath and called,
"Who are you?"

His only reply was the dreary hooting of an owl.
Ichabod shivered as he called again,
"WHO ARE YOU?"
Still no answer.

Just then, the monstrous shadow moved
to the middle of the road.
Although the night was dark and dismal,
Ichabod could see the monster's shape.
He appeared to be a giant rider
mounted on a powerful black horse.

As they rode to higher ground,
Ichabod saw the horseman
outlined against the sky.
He was enormous and wrapped in a cloak.
But Ichabod was struck with horror
when he saw that the rider had no head.
Yet more dreadful still —
if that were possible
was the sight of the head itself.
Instead of resting on the shoulders,
the head was carried before the horseman
on the pommel of the saddle.

Ichabod's teeth chattered,
and his fear turned to desperation.
He gave Gunpowder a kick in the ribs.
The horse snorted, but he would not run.
Indeed, he seemed to move more slowly.

The figure was coming nearer.
Ichabod could feel the hot breath
of the phantom steed close behind him.

Dizzy with fear, the schoolmaster rained
a shower of kicks and blows on Gunpowder
who suddenly broke into a gallop.
The phantom horse did the same.
Away they dashed,
over bushes and through brambles,
with stones flying at every turn.
The ride was so violent,
the schoolmaster felt
as if he were being torn apart.
To make matters worse,
the saddle slipped out from under him
and fell to the ground.

Ichabod grasped Gunpowder tightly around the neck
and forced himself to stay on the horse.
First he slid to one side, then the other.
Still, he didn't lose hope.
Through an opening in the trees,
he saw the haunted bridge,
famous in all the stories.
*If I can reach that bridge*, he thought,
*the ghost will vanish in a flash of fire.*

Ichabod heard the panting
of the monstrous phantom horse
and the crunching of dry leaves
beneath his gigantic hooves.
"Faster!" Ichabod whispered to Gunpowder.
After receiving another kick in the ribs,
the old horse sprang upon the bridge.
Thundering over the planks,
he finally reached the opposite side.

Then Ichabod looked back
to make sure the phantom had vanished
in a flash of fire.
But the phantom had not vanished.
Instead, he rose in his stirrups
and hurled his head at the schoolmaster.

Ichabod tried to dodge the horrible head,
but he was too late.
The hideous thing struck his skull
with a tremendous crash,
and Ichabod tumbled headlong into the dust.
Gunpowder, the phantom rider, and the black steed
passed him by like a whirlwind.

The following morning, Gunpowder was found
without his saddle, at his master's gate.
Ichabod was not seen at breakfast;
dinner hour came, still no Ichabod.
Students gathered at the school
and wandered near the brook,
but they couldn't find their schoolmaster.

Finally, after a long and thorough search,
the saddle was found trampled in the dirt.
Near the bridge,
they discovered Ichabod's woolen hat.
Close beside the hat
lay a shattered pumpkin.

The brook was searched,
but the schoolmaster's body was not found.
Indeed, the mysterious disappearance
of Ichabod Crane was never explained.
After considering many possibilities,
it was generally agreed
that he was carried off by the Headless Horseman.

However, several years later,
an old farmer visited New York City
and brought back some interesting news.
He'd heard that Ichabod was still alive.
Not only that, but he'd studied law,
become a politician,
and grown a bit stout.
It seemed that the schoolmaster had left Sleepy Hollow
not only because he'd lost Katrina,
but because of his fear of the Headless Horseman.

As for Brom Bones,
soon after his rival disappeared,
he led Katrina proudly to the altar.
And whenever he heard the story of Ichabod,
he always laughed heartily
at the mention of the pumpkin.
This made some people think
that Brom knew more than he chose to tell
about the disappearance of Ichabod Crane.

Nevertheless, the old country wives,
who know best about such matters,
insist that Ichabod was carried off
by the Headless Horseman.
To this very day,
they say the schoolmaster's voice
can be heard singing a melancholy tune
in the enchanted woodlands of Sleepy Hollow.

THE END